Last

Leaf

First

Snowflake

to

Fall

Leo Yerxa

Groundwood Books

House of Anansi Press

Toronto Berkeley

For Martin

Long ago, before time
Before sunlight burst across the universe
to give light to the heart of a dark green forest
Before that light broke into glistening sparkles
and was sent running and dancing across
oceans and raindrops by the gentlest of breezes

Before rain fell and became mud puddles and seas
and rose again to become clouds
to fall back to earth as rain again and again
Before forests had trees and trees had leaves
and leaves fell and trees fell
and trees grew and leaves grew and fell again
upon beds of moss made soft
for the first man to walk upon
Before chirpings, songs and whispers
brought joy to the forest
Before howling winds bid welcome
to the first snowflake
Before the scent of pine journeyed on the wind
linking heaven to earth, earth to man
man to eagle, eagle to spider
spider to bear and bear to heaven
and then melted back into the everything
Before raindrops washed spider webs and dust
Before the first stone skipped across water
shattering a mirrored image of the sky
Before shadows were placed
by the hands of the Creator
across rabbit trails on moonlit snow
Before the first man crushed dried leaves
beneath his feet, hurrying to who knows where
Before seeing, before being
Before valentines and wild flowers
Before fire and warmth
Before the eyes of the first man
watched the sun fall beneath the horizon
His eyes walked in darkness, from star to star
The first adventurers in the deep blue sky

From this darkness snow was born
It began with a whisper

from the wind to the leaves
the leaves to the birds

Startled, the birds flew south
Gone were their songs
All that remained was the silent warning
to gather food, to build shelters
to find the safe and secret place, and to sleep
Deer moved to high ground, fish to shallow waters
Squirrels gathered, man hunted
The wind sent shimmers of sunlight
across the dark waters of rivers and lakes
That is how fish were told of the snow
Wolves howled at the frozen moon
calling to the last cry of the loon
The great bear yawned
Squirrels dashed through leaves
Mice hurried across rocky ledges
The last duck raced across the dark sky

I touched the frost on the window with my nose
The frost melted away, forming a tiny hole
I pressed my eye to the hole and looked to the sky
My eye walked in darkness, from star to star
The first light found its way through the forest
through the frosted window and across my face
A new day began

Dried leaves shattered beneath our feet
We hurried through the darkness of the forest
A flock of geese drifted across the sky
They weaved their way from dark blue patches
to patches of clouds, then they fell
beneath the horizon
We walked to the shore where our canoe sat waiting

The sky gave its colors to the water
It was as if our canoe was drifting across the sky
The far shore did not reveal its mysteries
of passageways, bays, creeks and ponds
Hidden in the colors lay a beaver's pond

The pond was silent and
   surrounded by fallen
   trees
It had a peace not given to
   any other part of the
   forest
A squirrel announced our
   arrival with its chirping
Twigs and leaves floated in
   the water
A leaf floated in the air and
   finally rested on the
   pond
creating a tiny circle that
   grew and grew
until the circle was the
   same size as the pond

Light winds scattered leaves onto the water
and into our canoe
We paddled to an island
Here we would make a fire and eat

S unlight stole through the trees

Playing, rolling on the ground, I was a leaf

W e moved on

We walked inland, along rocky ledges
up hills covered with fallen trees
and on logs suspended across creeks

We walked until we came to a swamp
There was no silence here
Dead trees creaked back and forth
Tall grass twisted with the wind
A squirrel gave its usual warning
Sticks cracked — a deer, maybe
A swamp speaks in many ways
Tracks told of visitors
deer, moose, mink, otter and fisher
and the tracks of many other animals could be seen
We were the only nishnawbe to visit this secret place

We left the swamp
Our footprints mingled the dried leaves and wet mud
and they would tell the other animals
of our visit to the swamp

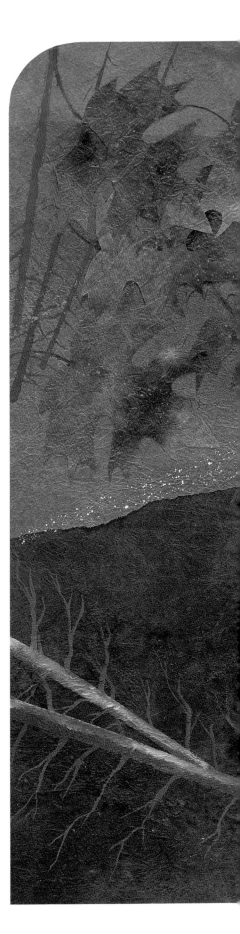

The winds grew colder,
the sky grew darker

It was the time now to rest
We made a fire
Our canoe was tilted and used as a shelter from rain or snow
The night wind howled a warning
The moon and stars were swallowed up by dark clouds
The last leaf fell
I closed my eyes and fell asleep
From the darkness the first snowflake fell

Night passed

M orning came

The blanket of leaves that yesterday covered the earth
was now covered with a blanket of snow
to keep her warm during her long winter sleep
My blanket was also covered in snow
I brushed the snow away
Gone were the colors of yesterday
I arose from the earth
and walked into the light
of a new season

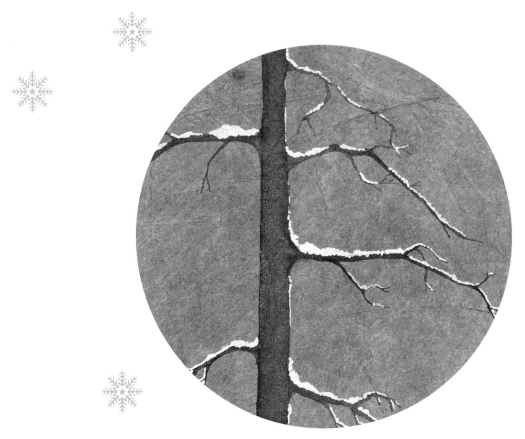

NOTE: Nishnawbe, or Anishnawbe, means people.

The artist would like to thank the Canada Council for its generous assistance.

Groundwood Books / House of Anansi Press
110 Spadina Avenue, Suite 801, Toronto, Ontario M5V 2K4
or c/o Publishers Group West
1700 Fourth Street, Berkeley, CA 94710

We acknowledge for their financial support of our publishing program the Canada Council for the Arts, the Government of Canada through the Canada Book Fund (CBF) and the Ontario Arts Council.

 Canada Council   Conseil des Arts
for the Arts   du Canada

 ONTARIO ARTS COUNCIL
CONSEIL DES ARTS DE L'ONTARIO

Library and Archives Canada Cataloguing in Publication
Yerxa, Leo
Last leaf first snowflake to fall / Leo Yerxa
A poem.
ISBN 978-1-55498-124-3
I. Title.
PS8597.E77L3 2012   jC811'.54   C2012-900741-2

The collage illustrations are done in tissue paper dyed with acrylics, inks and watercolor. The small accent illustrations are in watercolor.

Design by Michael Solomon
Printed and bound in China